Fairy House

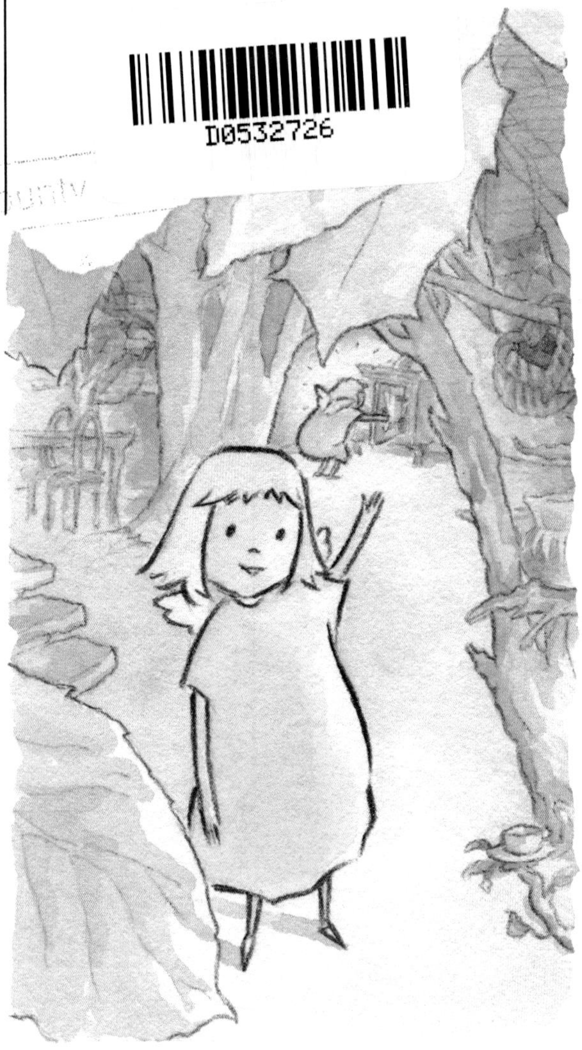

Sally Barton

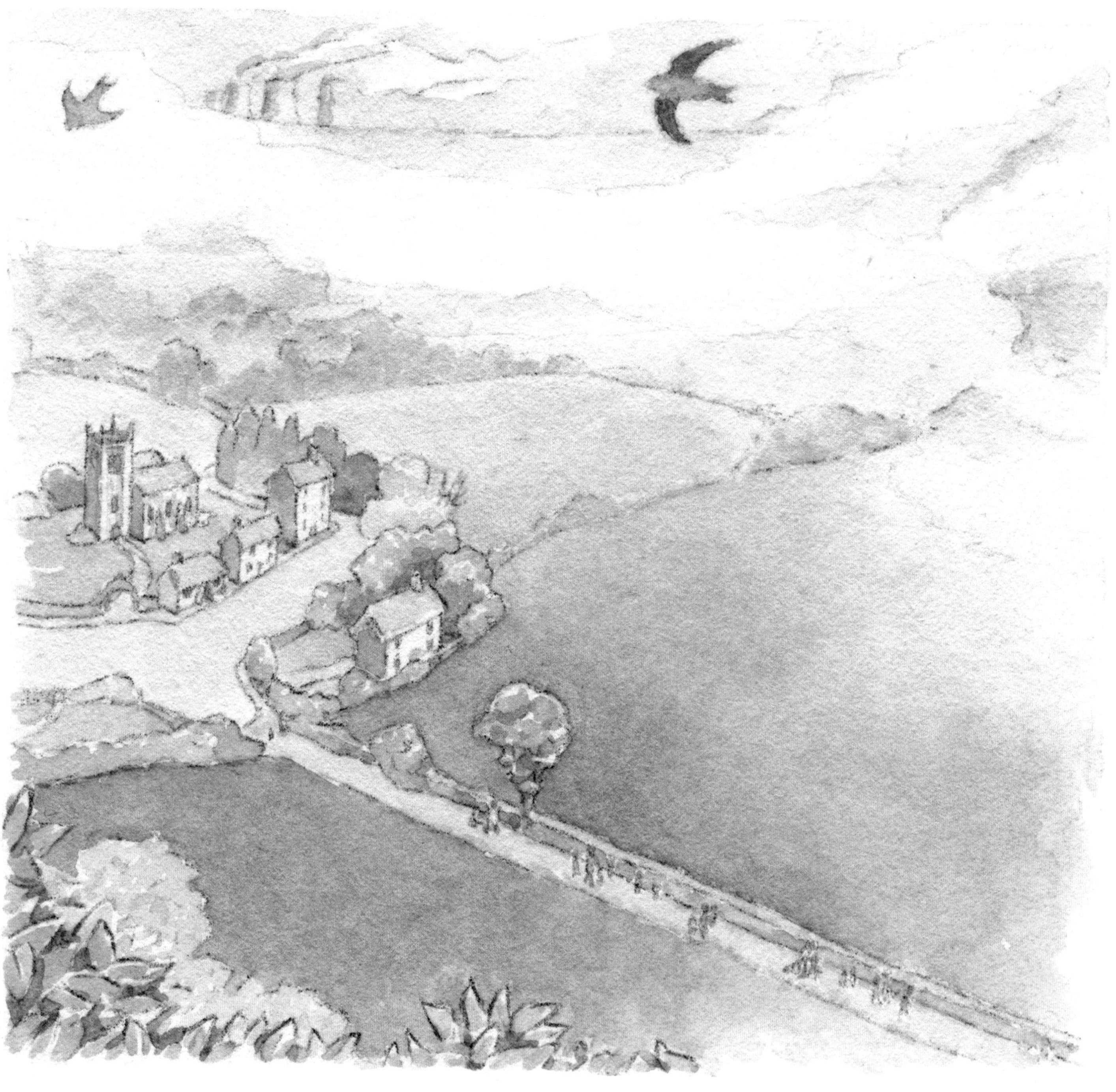

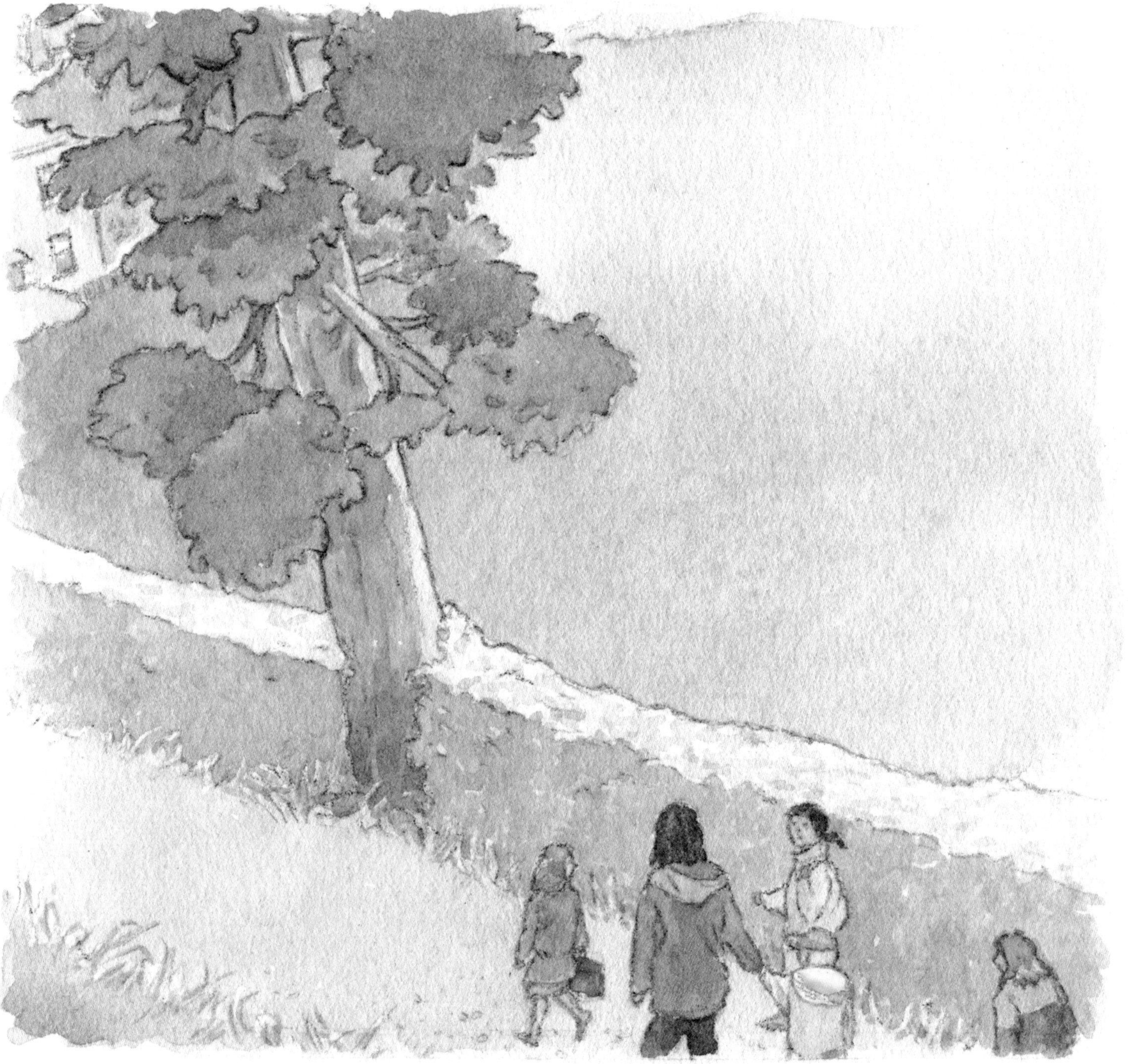

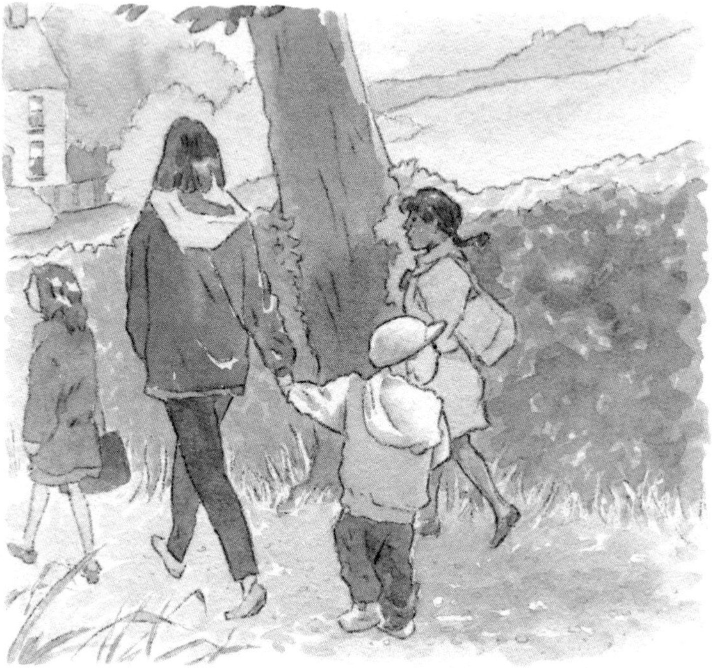

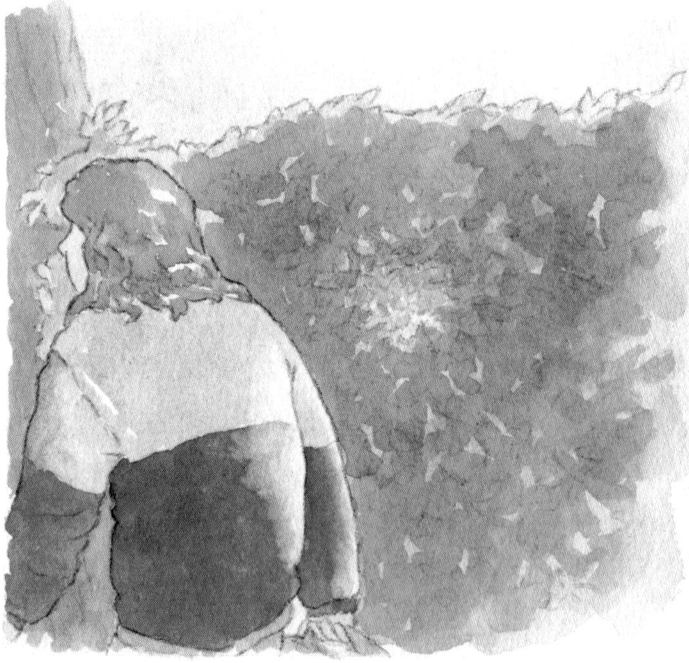

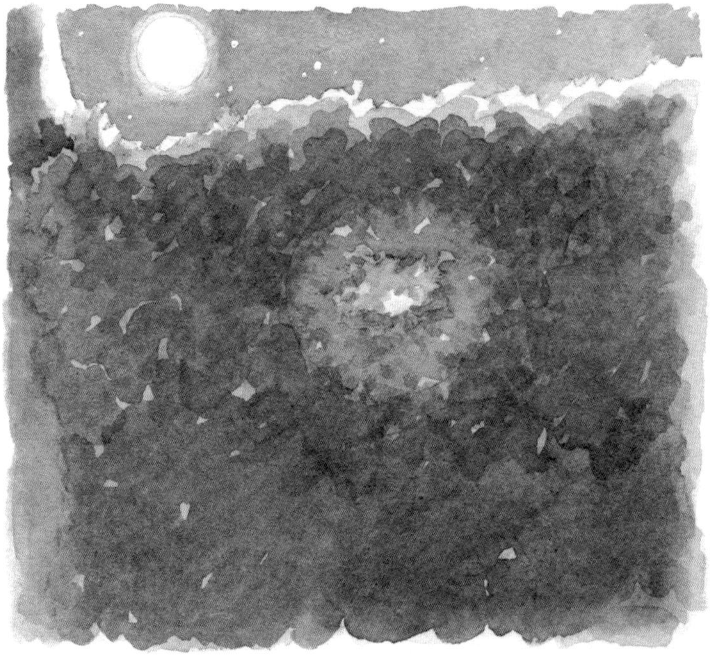

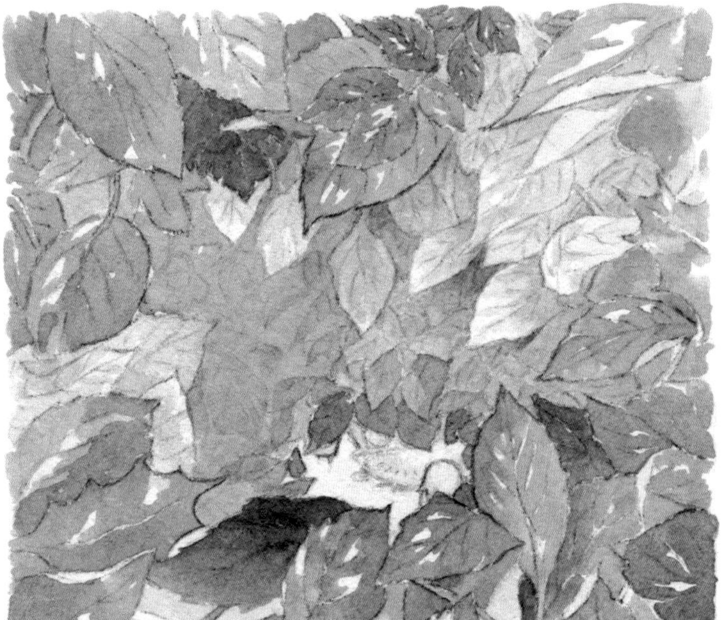

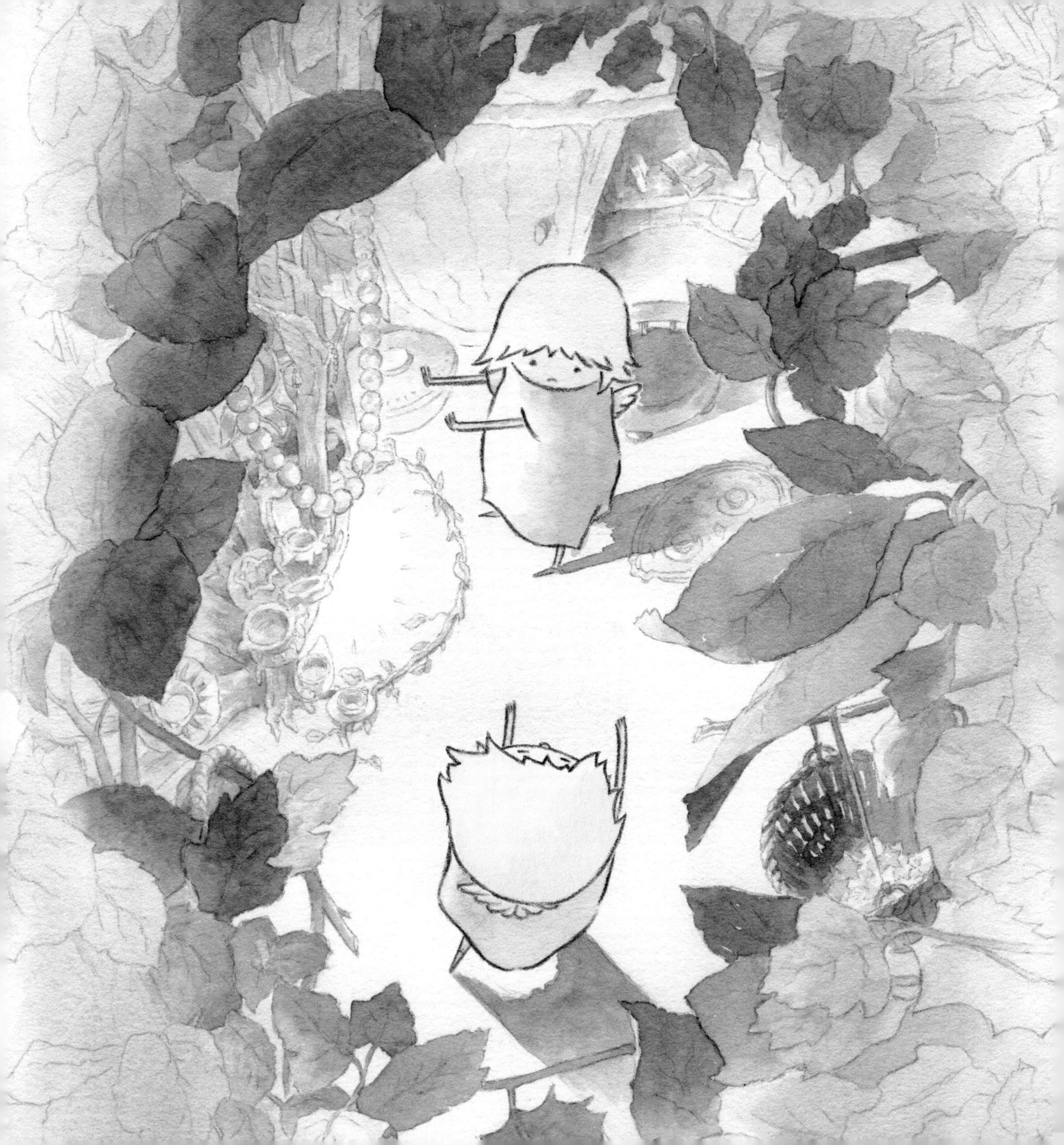

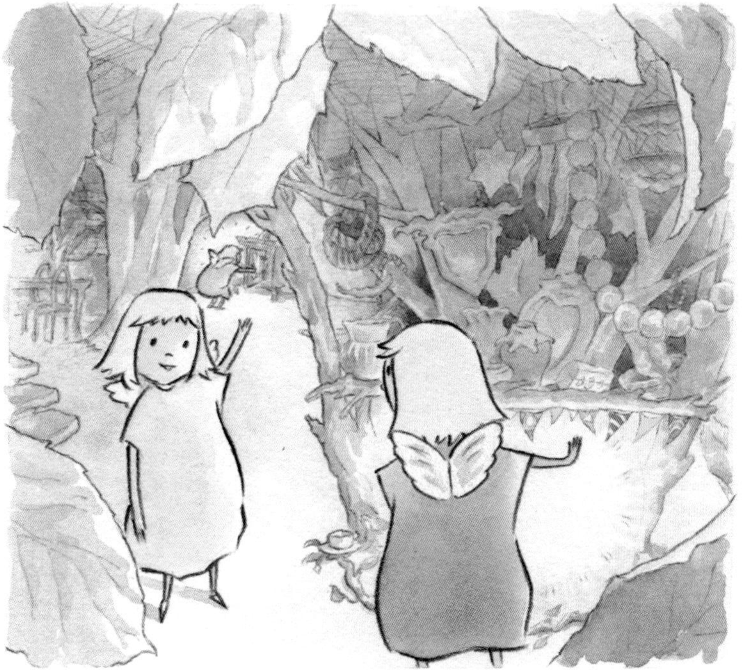

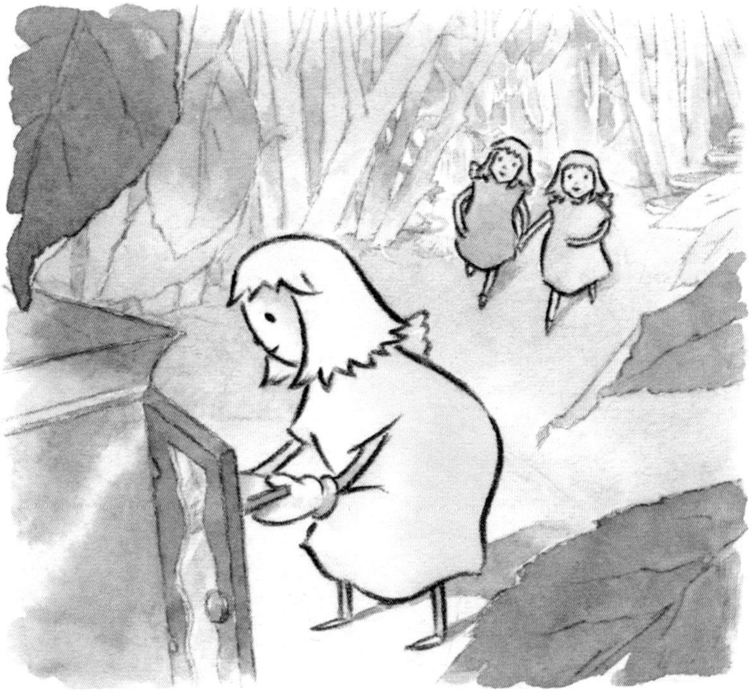

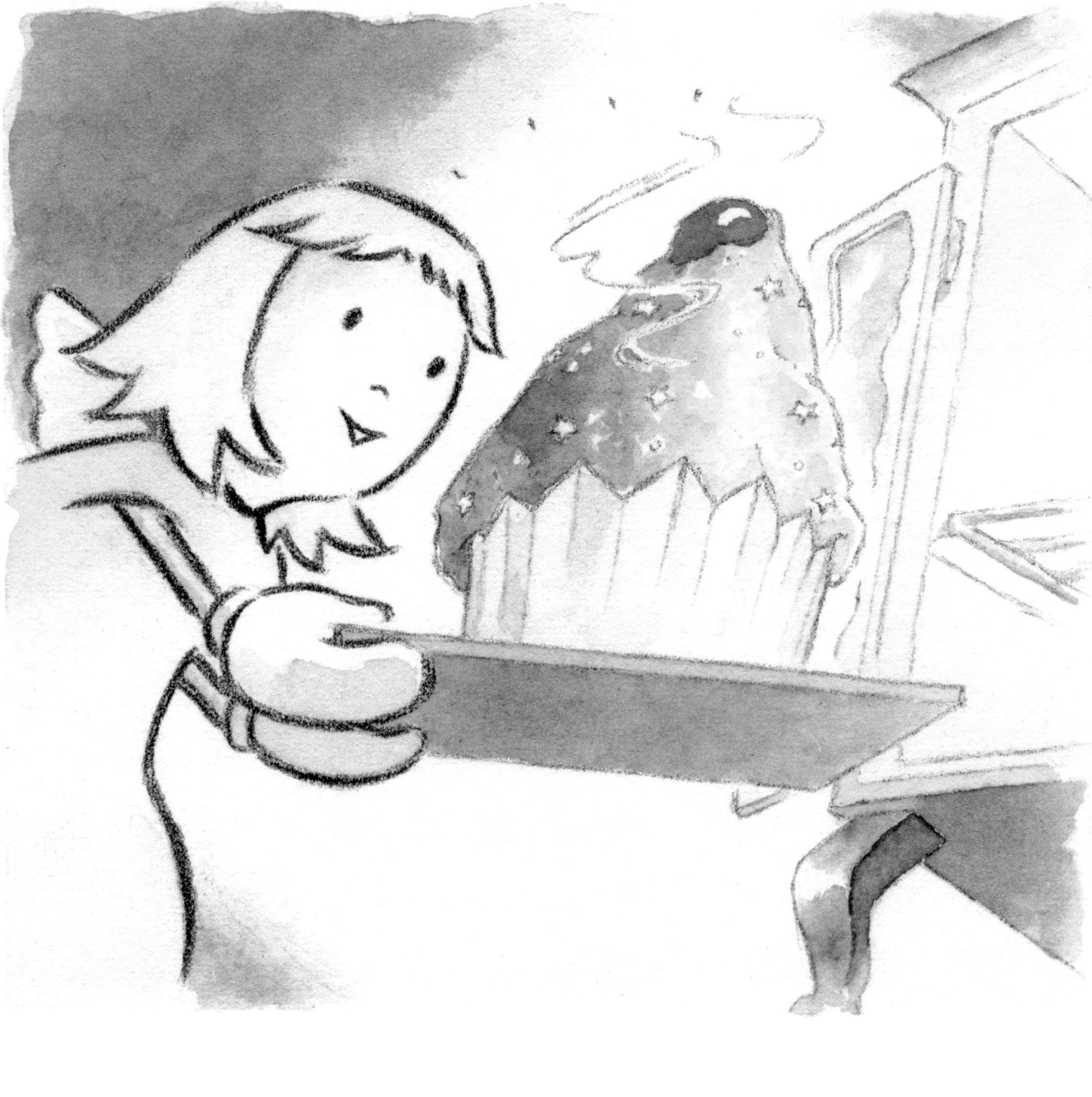

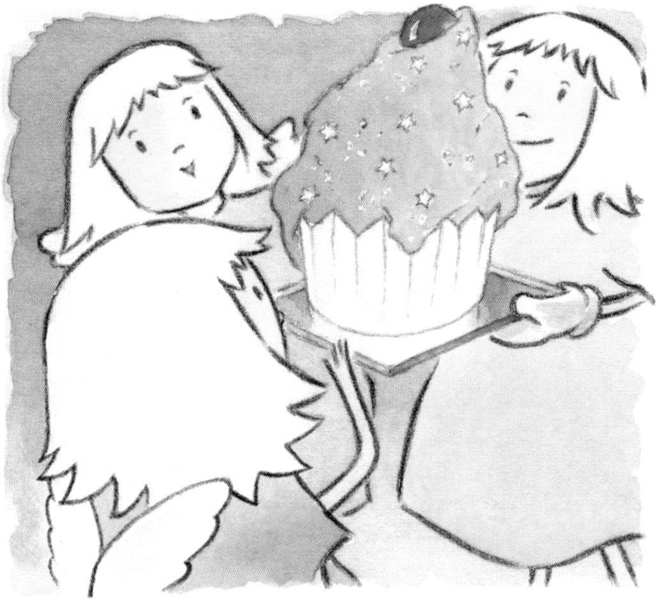
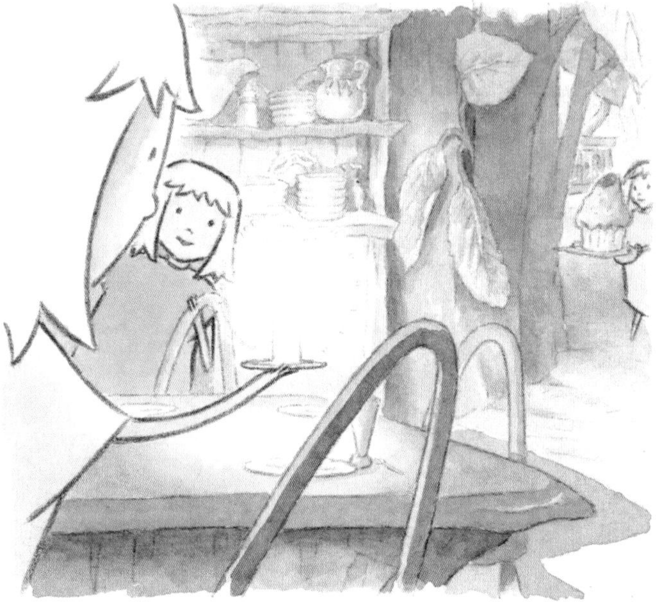
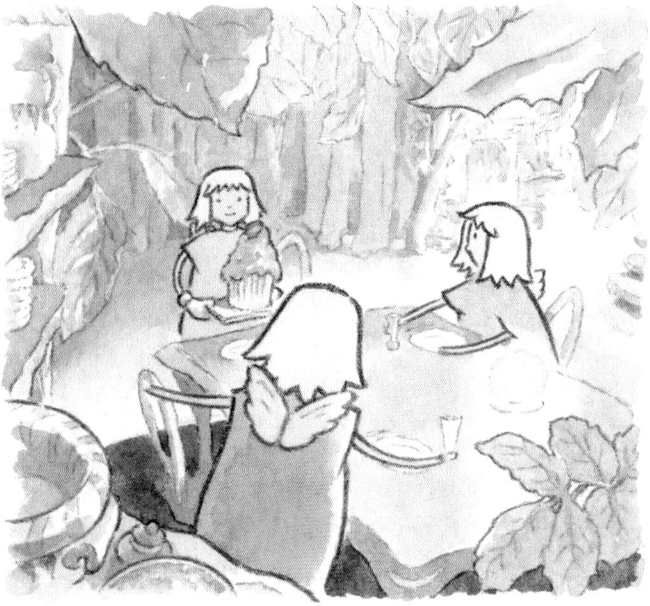
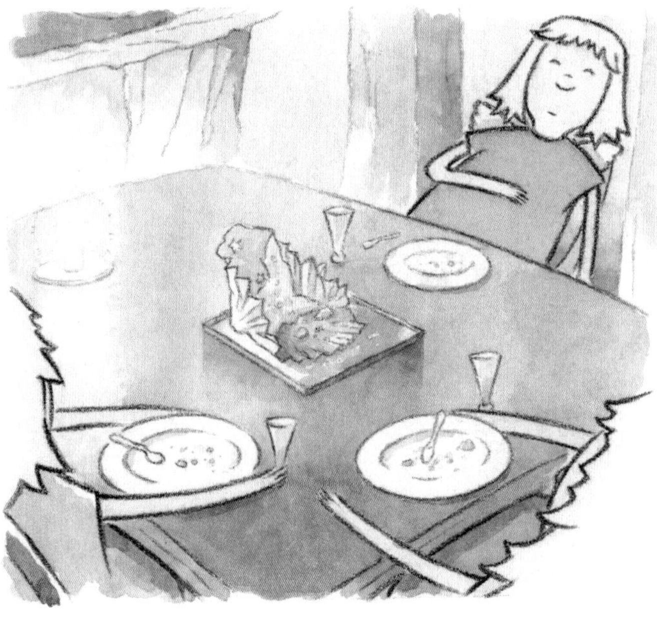

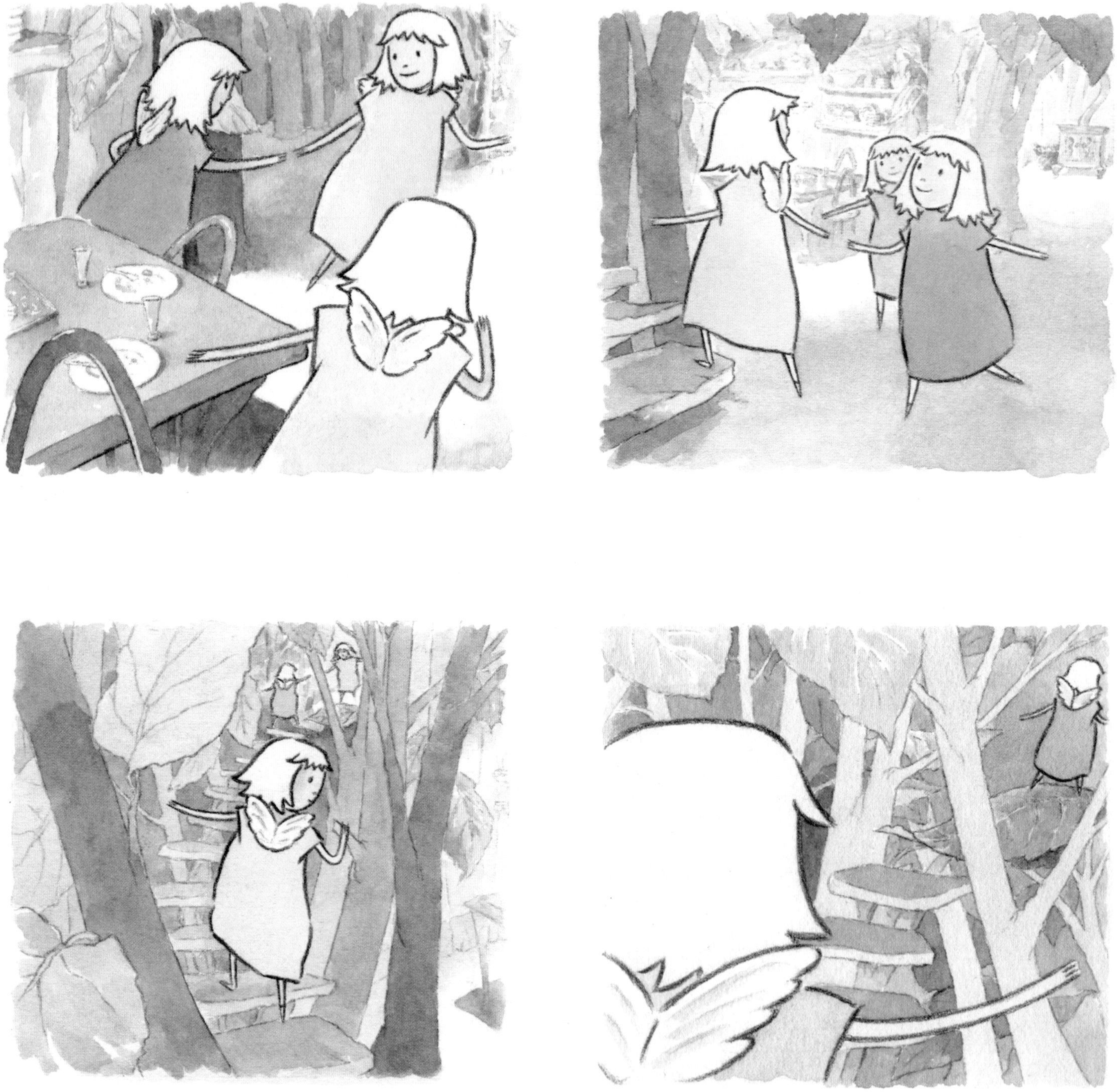

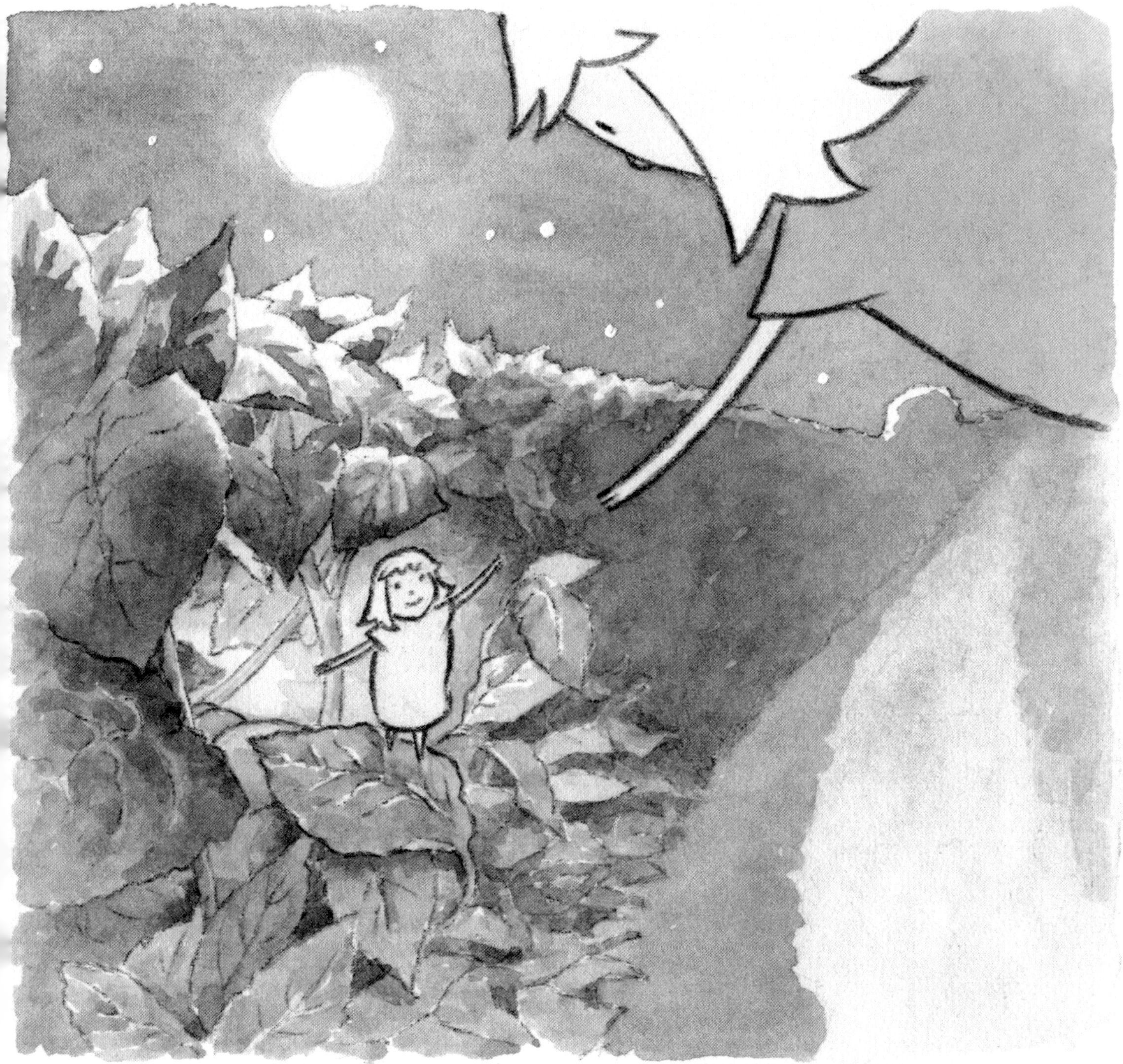

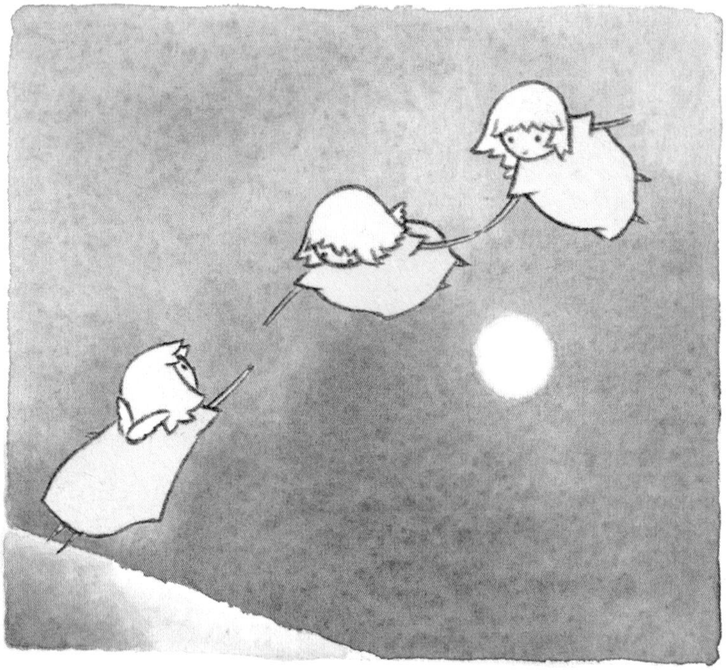
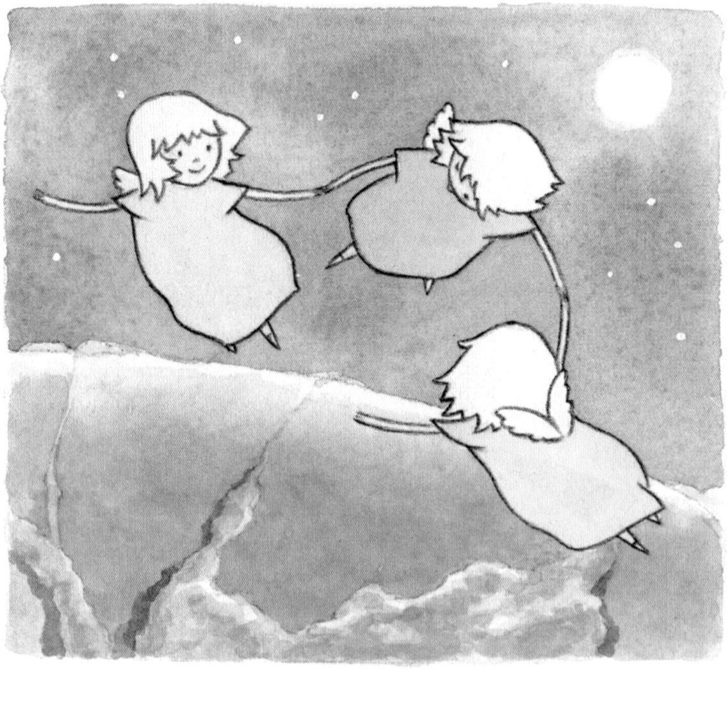

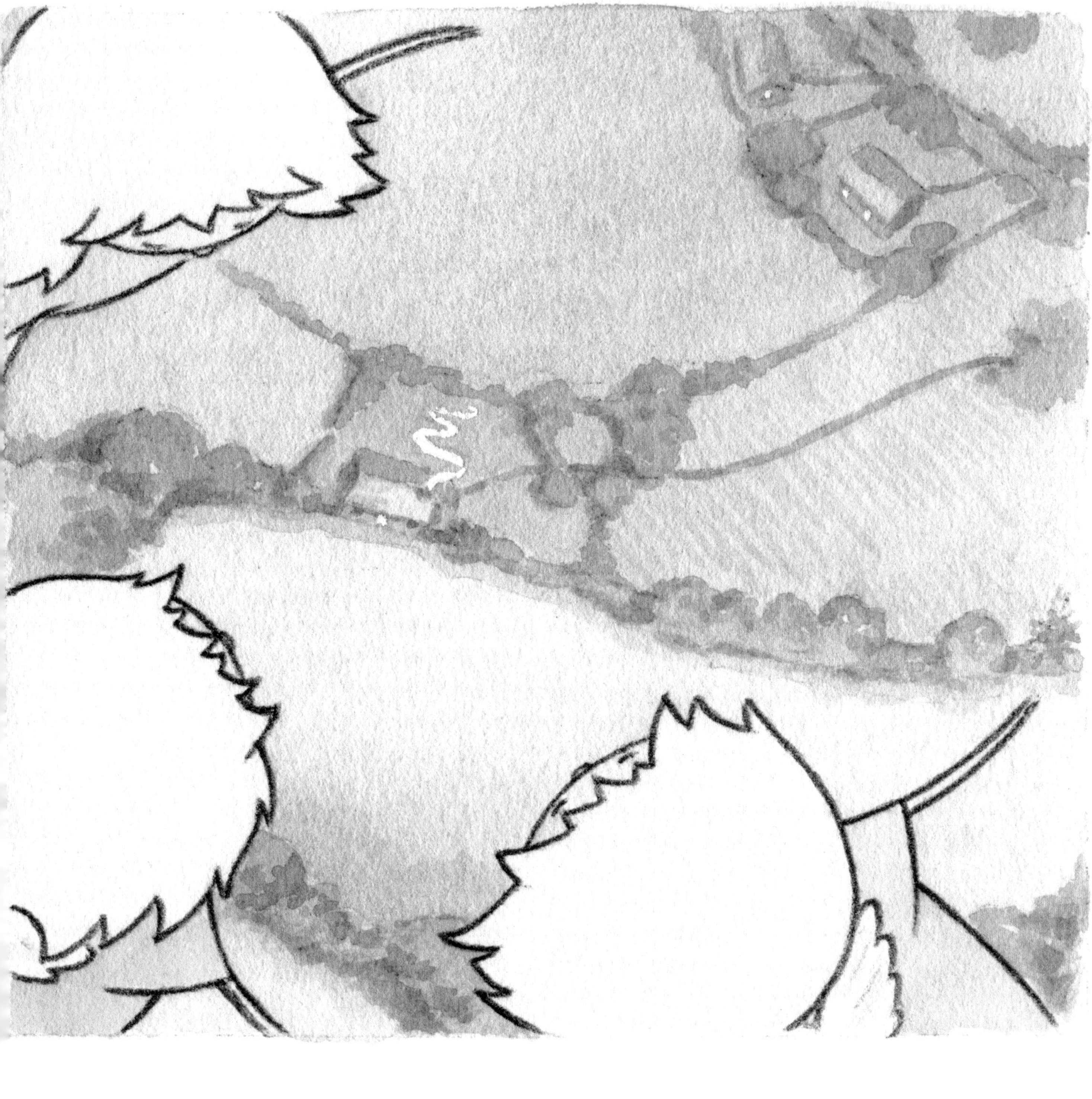

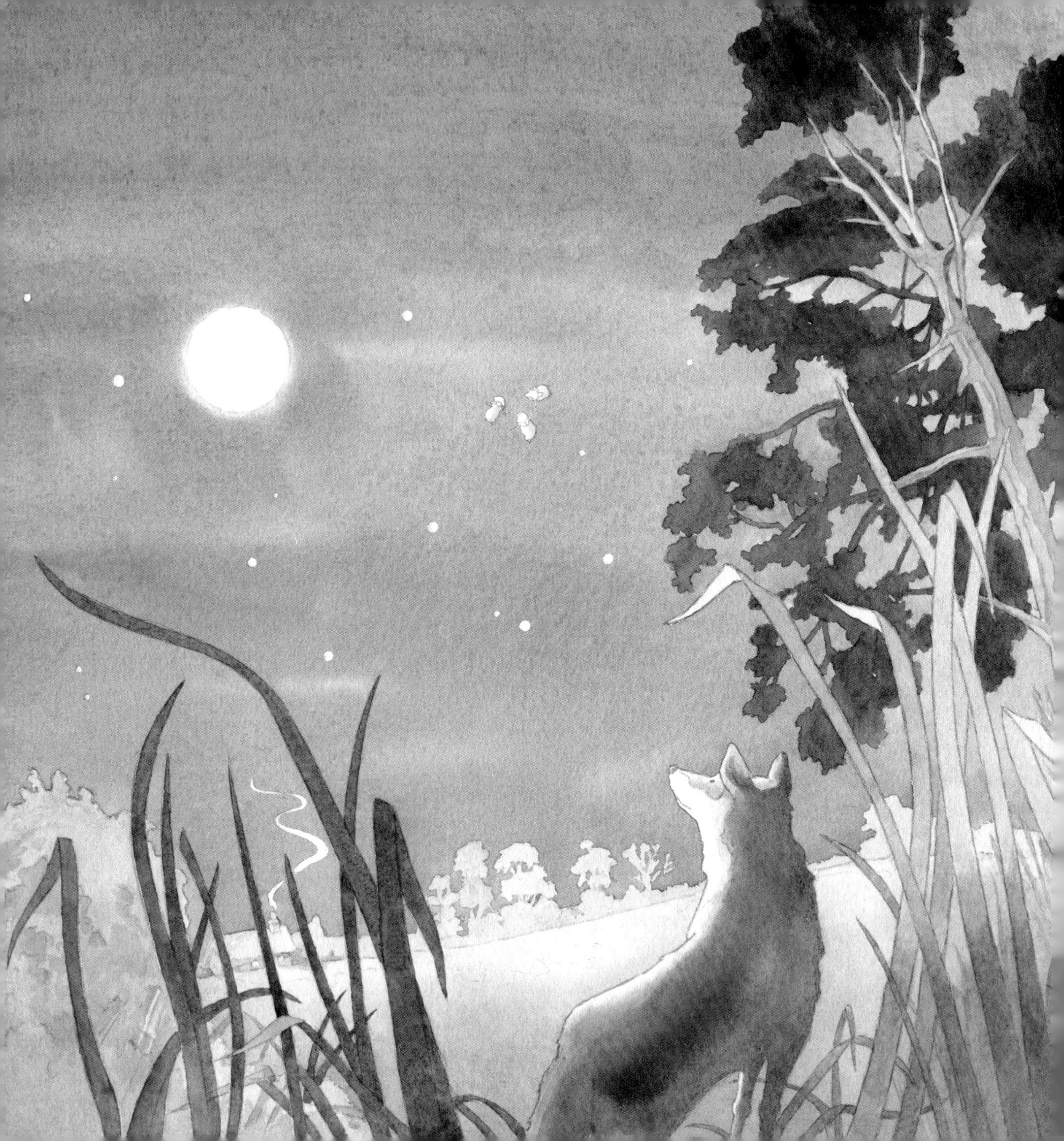

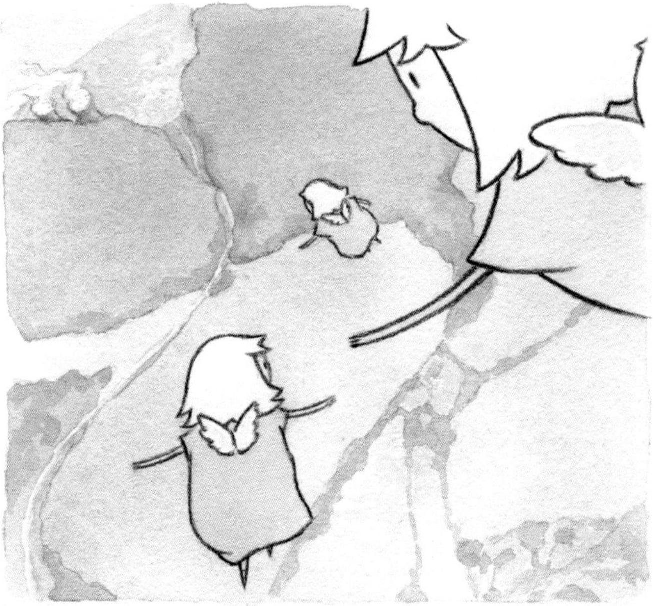
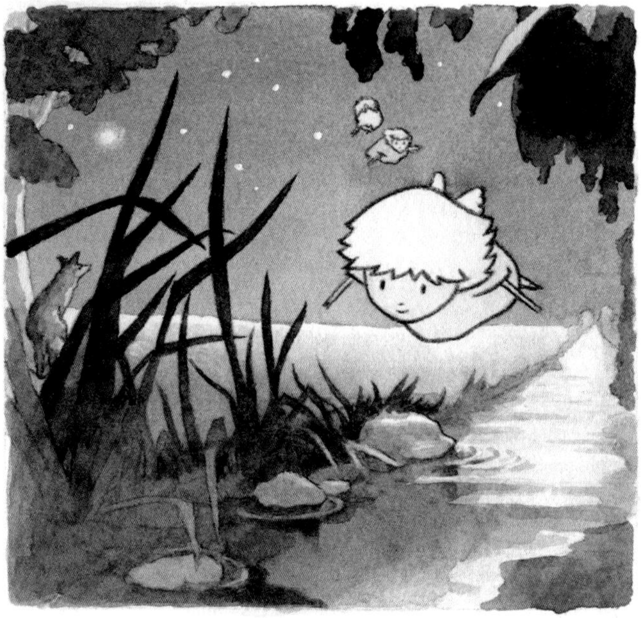
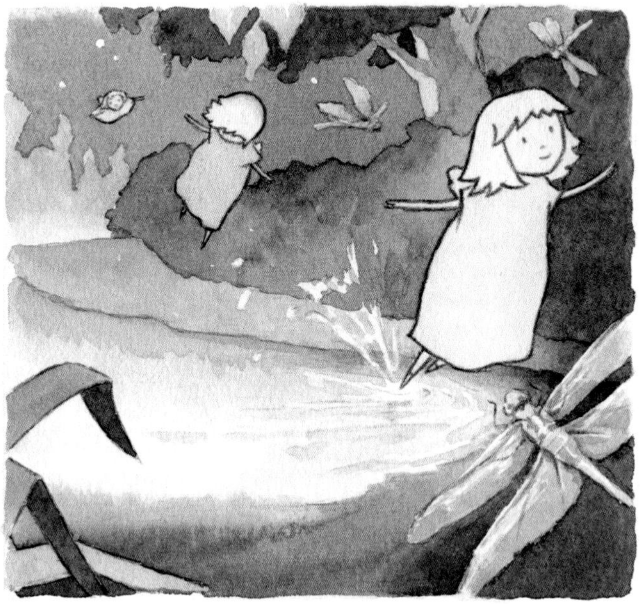
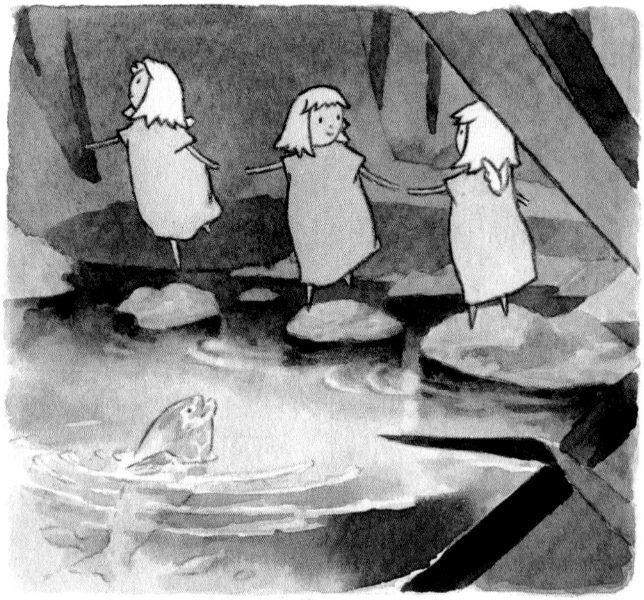

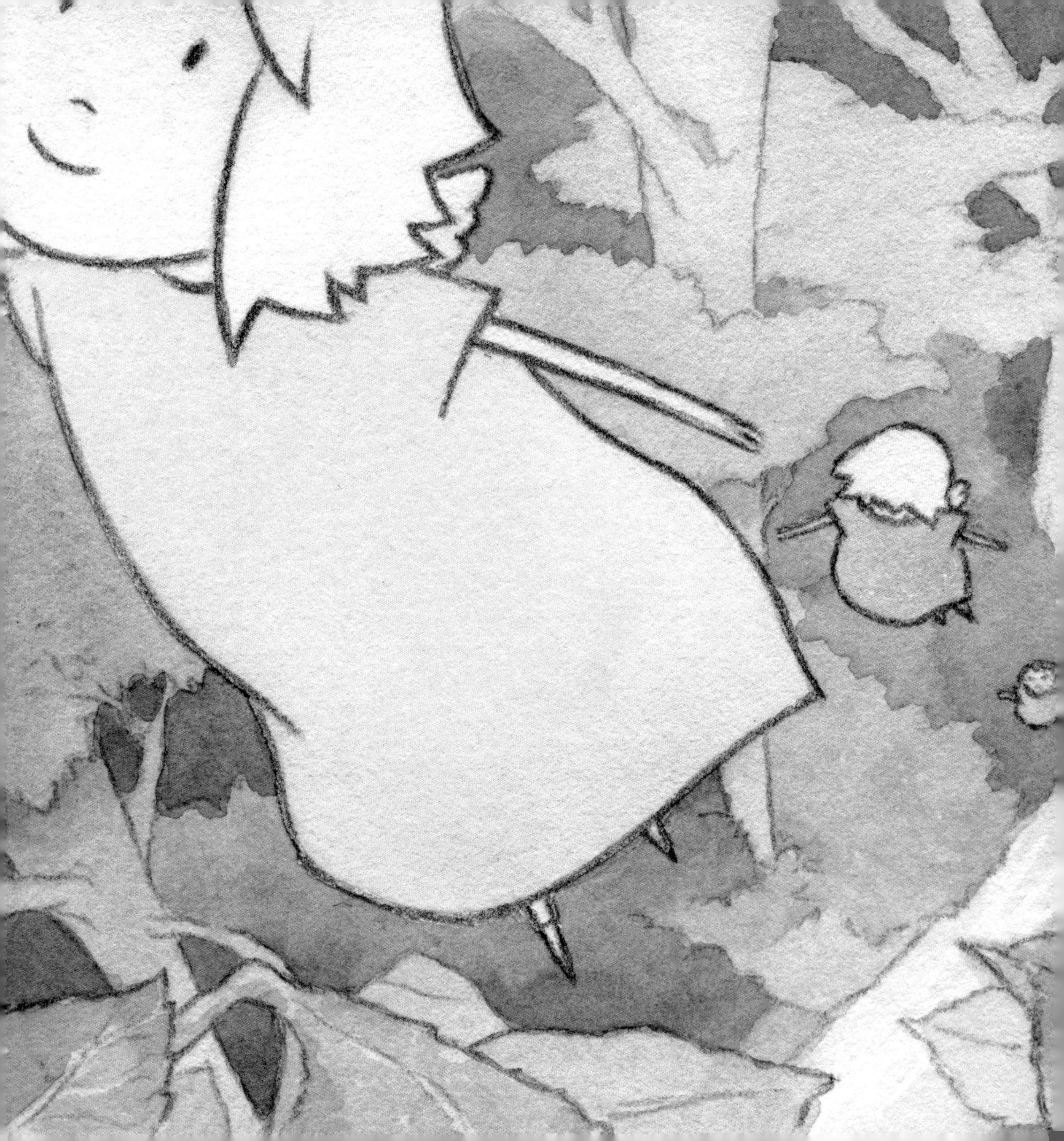

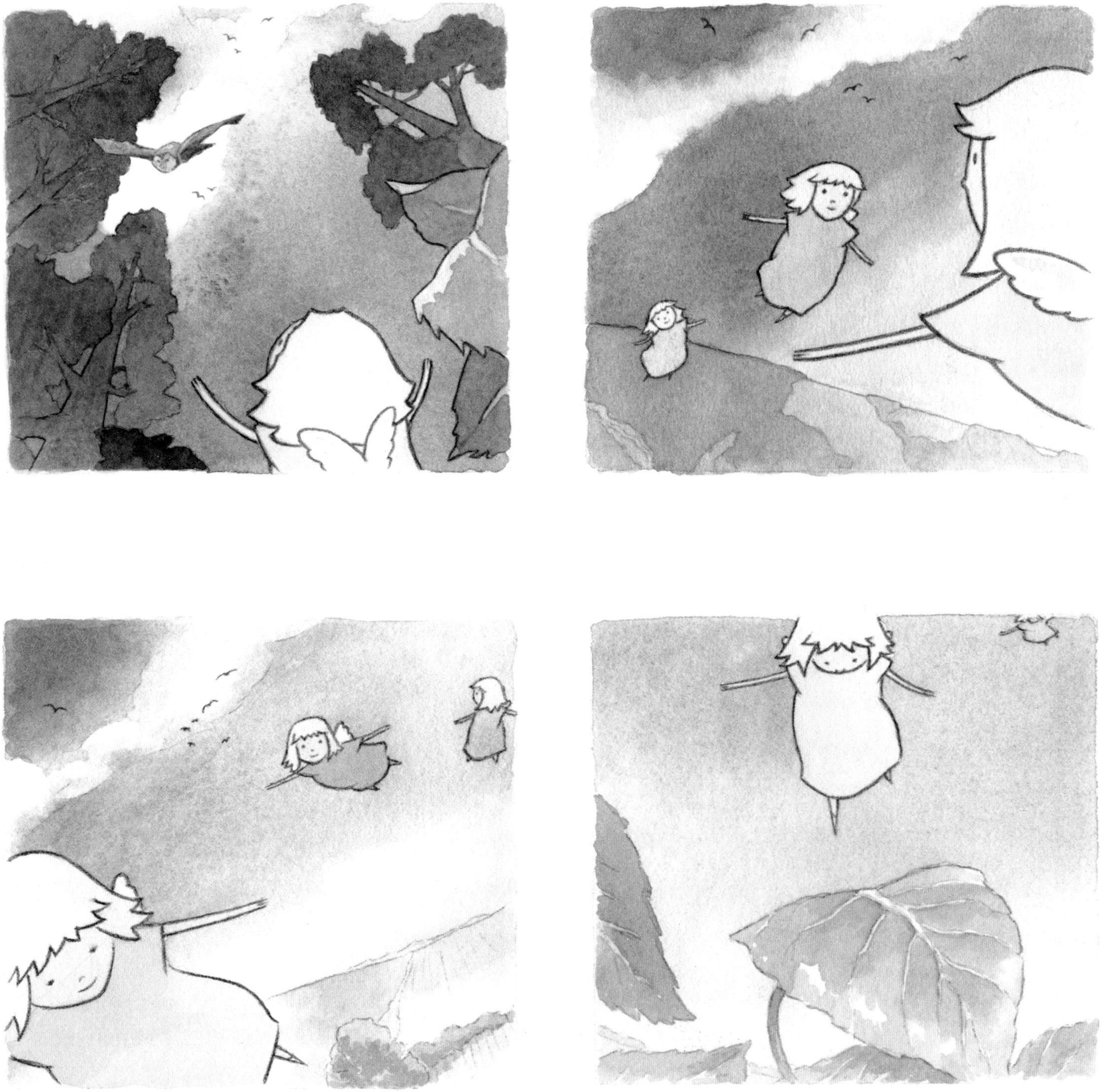

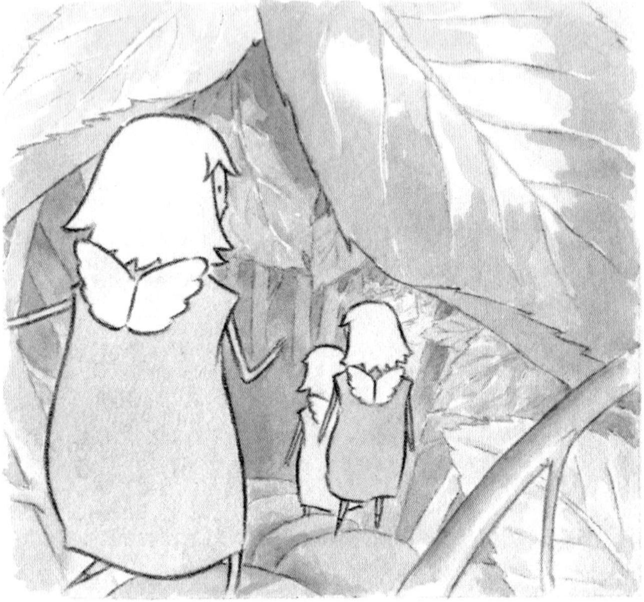
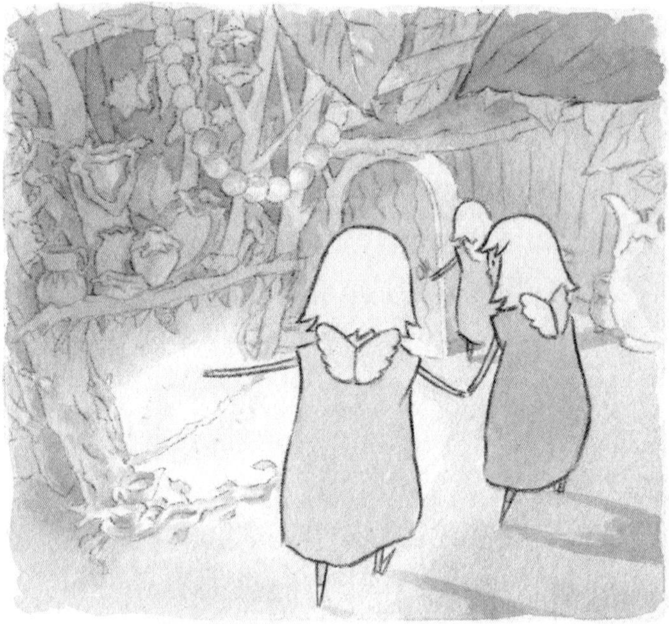
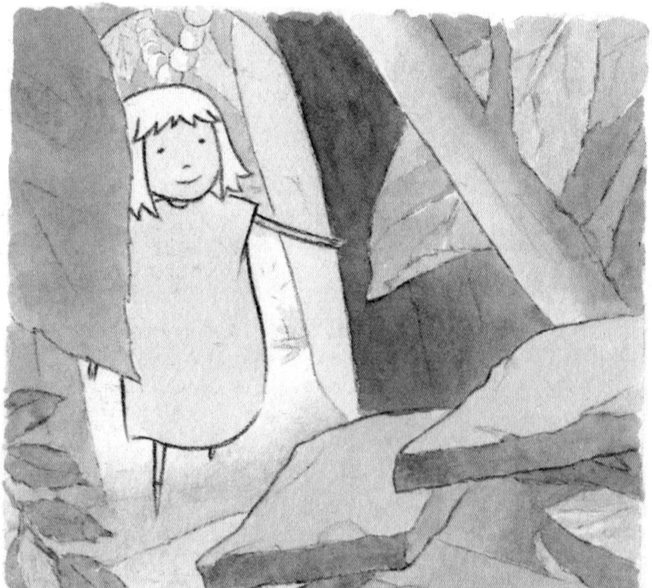
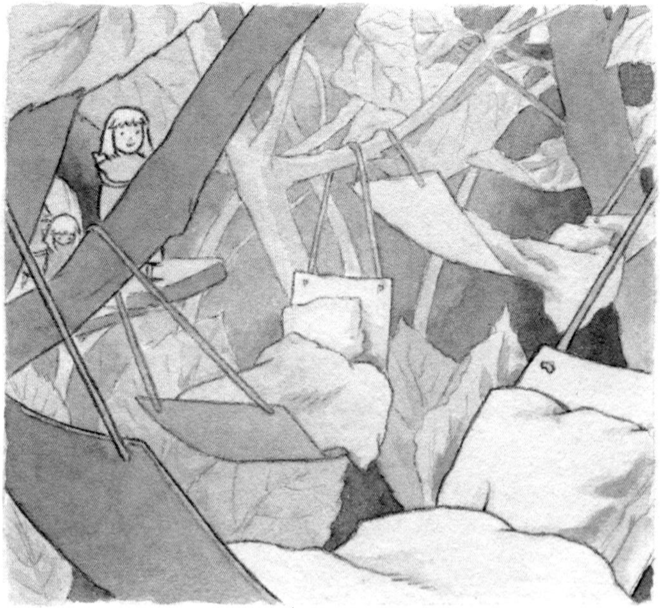

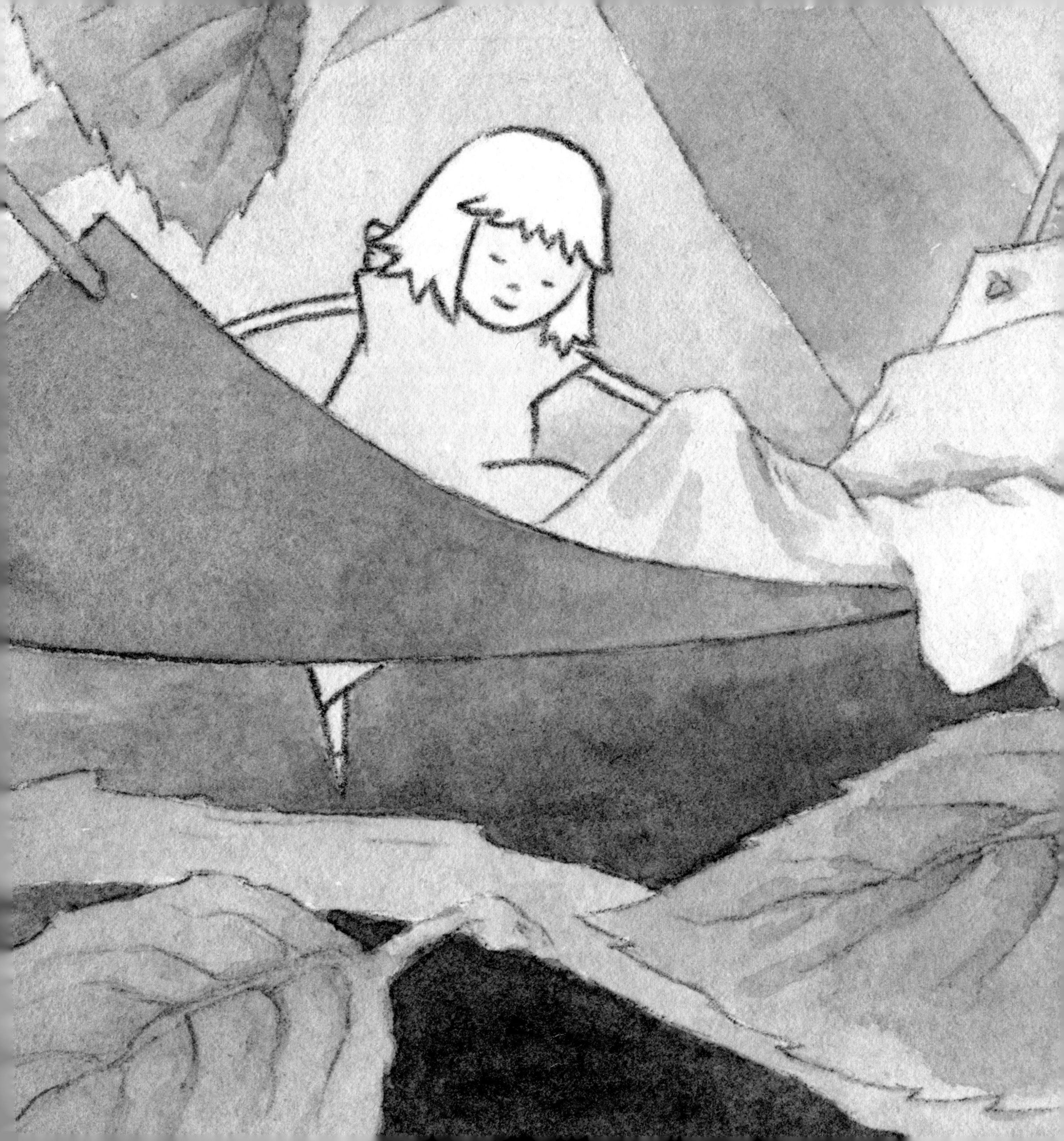

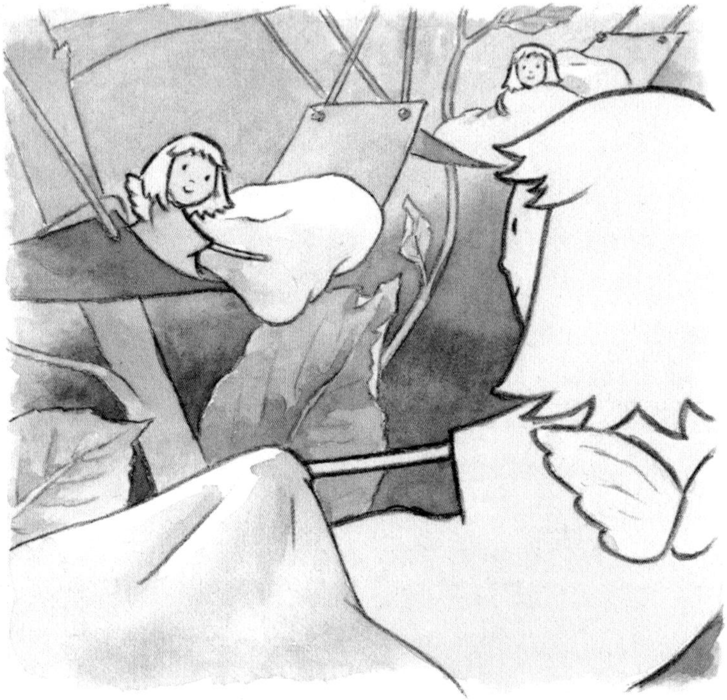

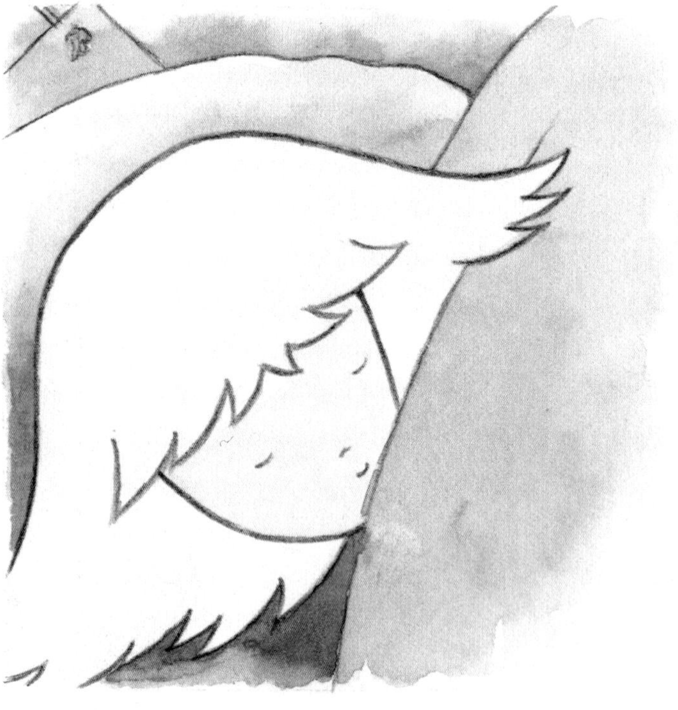

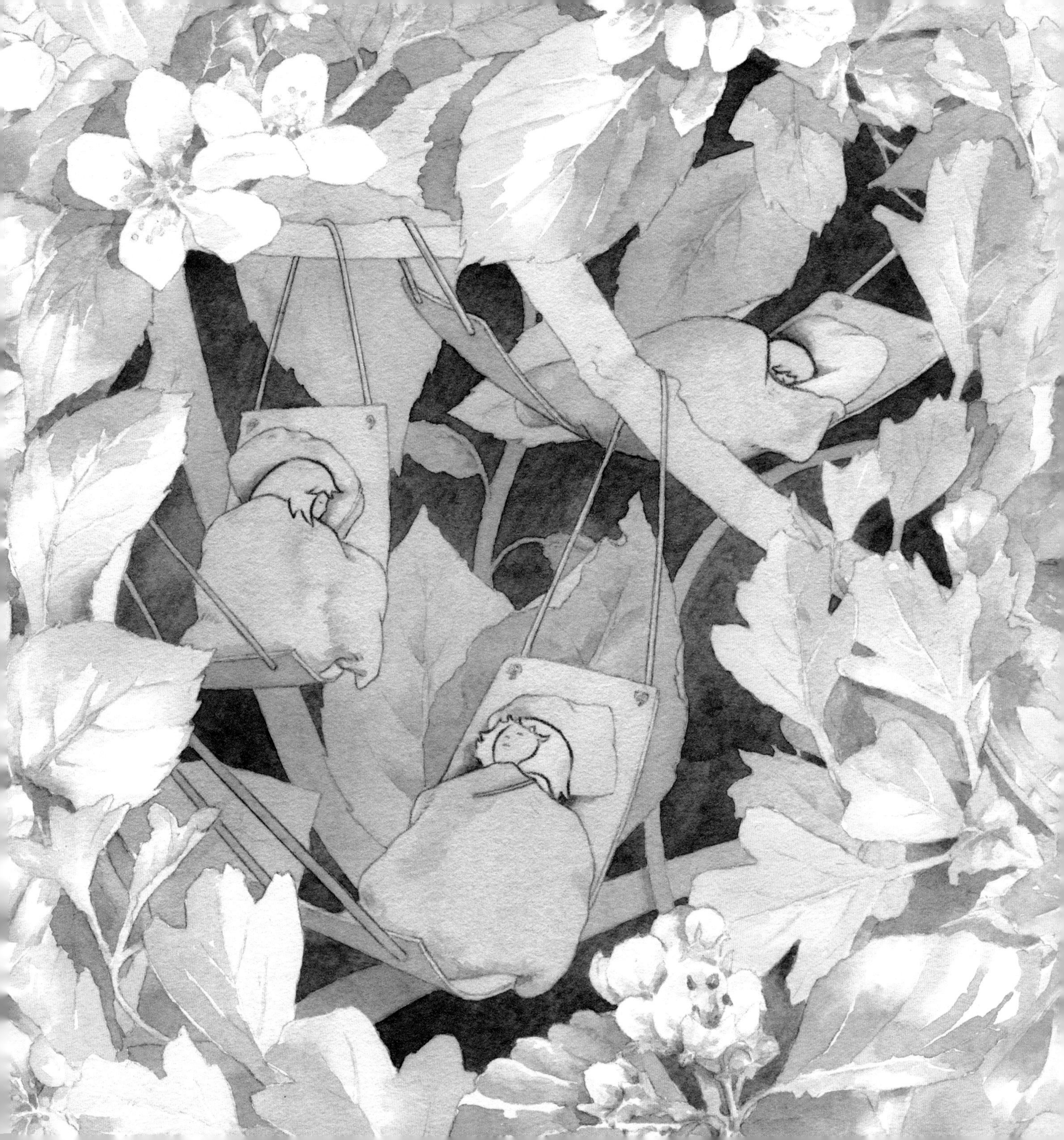

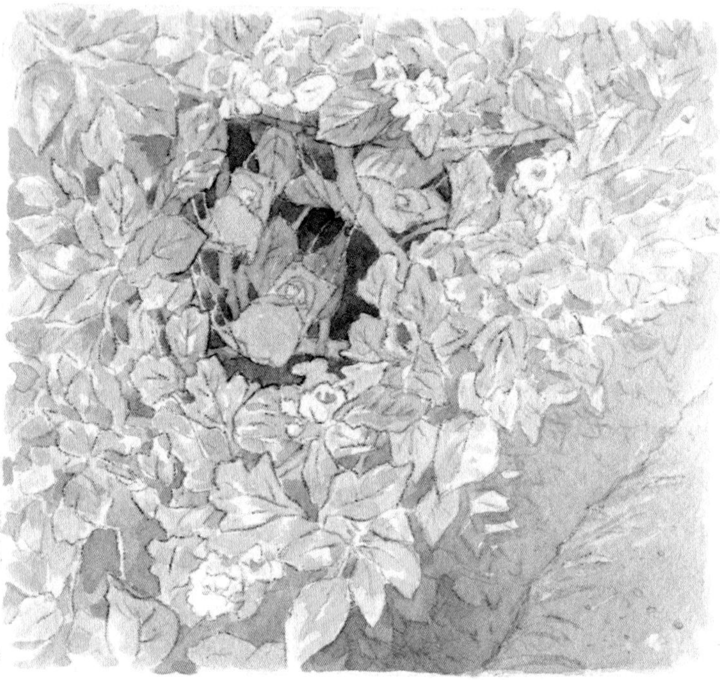

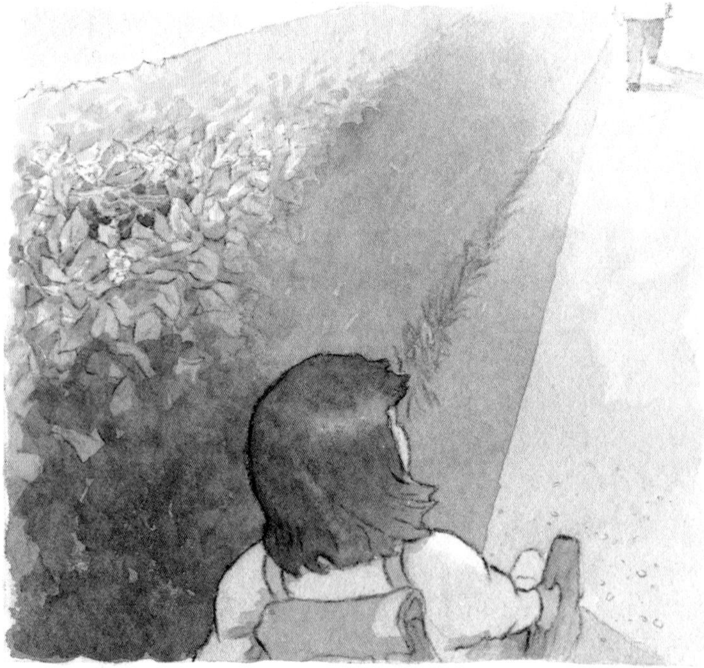

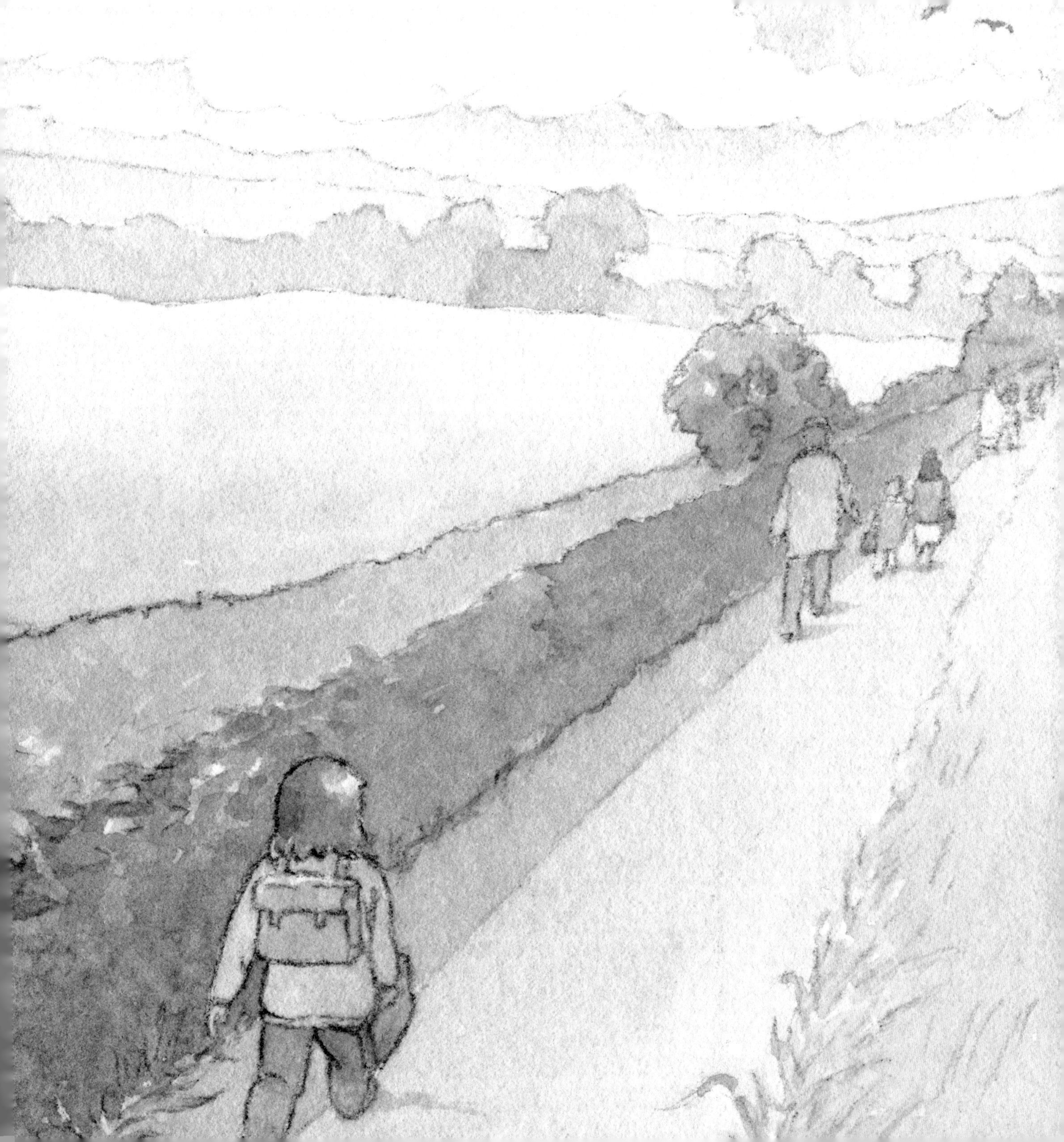

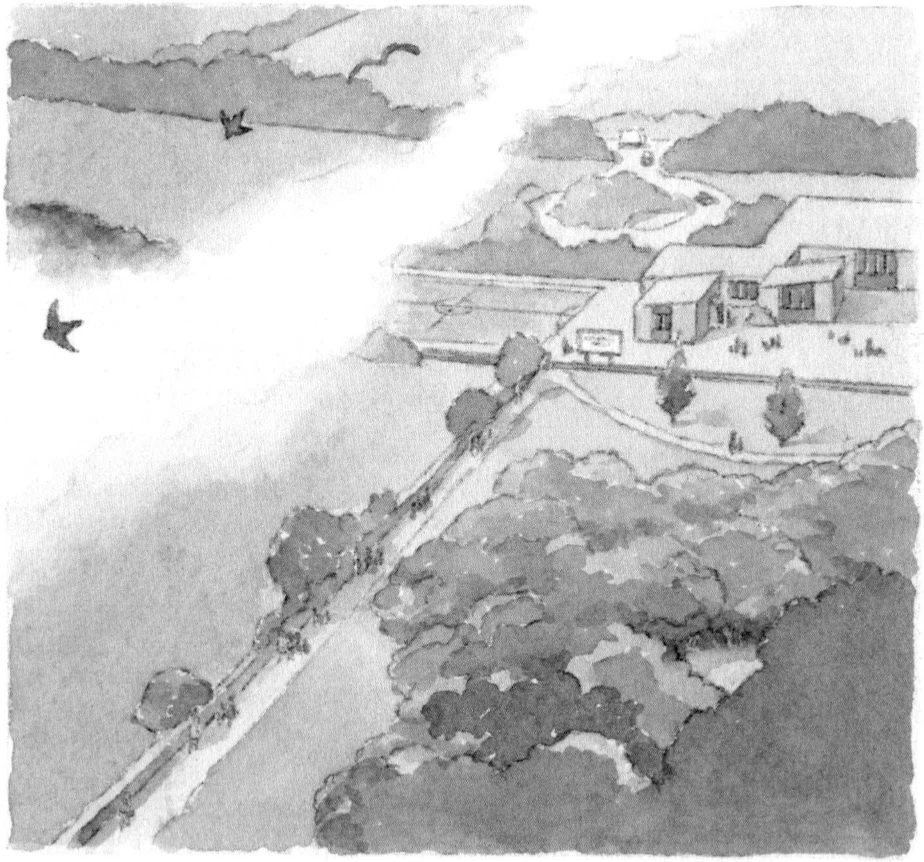